My Bedtime Collection of
★ First Favorite ★
Tales

©LADYBIRD BOOKS LTD MM
The Three Billy Goats Gruff illustrations © Sam Childs
Published and Distributed by
Flying Frog Publishing, Inc.
An imprint of Allied Publishing Group, Inc.
ISBN 1-57755-277-6
Printed in China

My Bedtime Collection of

★ First Favorite ★
Tales

Ladybird

Introduction

A perfect first collection of timeless and treasured stories, with amusing pictures and rhymes, will delight young children everywhere.

Contents

Goldilocks and the Three Bears

based on a traditional folk tale
retold by Nicola Baxter
illustrated by Liz Pichon

LIttle Gingerbread Man

based on a traditional folk tale
retold by Alan MacDonald
illustrated by Anja Rieger

The Little Red Hen

based on a traditional folk tale
retold by Ronnie Randall
illustrated by Liz Pichon

The Three Billy Goats Gruff

based on a traditional folk tale
retold by Irene Yates
illustrated by Sam Childs

The Three Little Pigs

based on a traditional folk tale
retold by Nicola Baxter
illustrated by Jan Lewis

Goldilocks
and the
Three Bears

Deep in the forest lived three bears.
There was **BIG** Father Bear,

middle-sized Mother Bear,

and tiny little
Baby Bear.

Father Bear had a **BIG** voice. Mother Bear had a middle-sized voice. Baby Bear had a tiny little voice. You could only just hear it.

Bright and early one morning, Mother Bear was busy making breakfast.

"We'll enjoy our porridge even more if we have a little walk first," said Father Bear.

Best paws forward!

Off we go!

But while the bears were walking, so was someone else. It was a little girl called…

…Goldilocks.

She had golden hair, and her cheeks were rosy. But little Goldilocks was rather nosy!

When she saw the house, with the door open wide, that naughty little girl walked right inside!

I smell porridge!

Goldilocks was feeling curious. There on the table she saw three bowls of porridge, so she picked up a spoon to have a taste.

The first bowl of porridge was much too hot.

The second bowl was much too lumpy!

But, "Mmmmm!" The third little bowl of porridge was just right… and suddenly it was absolutely empty!

Feeling rather full and sleepy, Goldilocks looked for a chair.

How many do you think were standing there?

The first chair was much too hard.

The second chair was much too soft!

But the third little chair was just right – for a baby bear. Goldilocks sat down and...

...CRASH! She smashed the little chair.

Goldilocks felt tired and upset after such a bruising bump. She quickly hurried up the stairs and peeked into the…

…bedroom.

There she saw a **BIG** bed, a middle-sized bed and a tiny little cozy bed.

The first bed was much too hard.

The second bed was much too soft!

But, "Mmmmm!" The third little bed was just right…

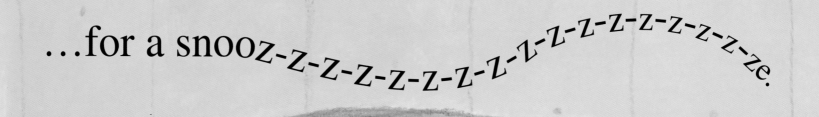

...for a snooz-z-z-z-z-z-z-z-z-z-z-z-z-ze.

Meanwhile on the forest track, the three bears were coming back.

They noticed right away that things were wrong.

I smell trouble!

"Someone's been eating my porridge!"
growled Father Bear.

"Someone's been eating my porridge!"
said Mother Bear.

"Someone's been eating my porridge," squeaked Baby Bear, "and they've eaten it all up!"

"Someone's been sitting in MY chair!" growled Father Bear.

"Someone's been sitting in *my* chair!" said Mother Bear.

"Someone's been sitting in my chair, too," sobbed Baby Bear.

He was the saddest bear of all. There was nothing left of his little chair.

Quietly on their furry paws, the bears crept slowly up the stairs.

"Someone's been sleeping in MY bed!" grunted Father Bear.

"Someone's been sleeping in *my* bed!" said Mother Bear.

"Someone's been sleeping in my bed," squeaked Baby Bear...

"…and she's still there!"

Baby Bear's tiny voice woke Goldilocks.
She opened one eye… and then the other…

Then she jumped out of bed, ran out of the house, and never went back.

And what's more, after that Goldilocks never had porridge for breakfast!

The Gingerbread Man

One morning a baker said to his wife, "Today I'll bake a gingerbread man. He'll look just right in our shop window."

So the baker made a gingerbread man
and put him in the oven. Before long they
heard a noise. A little voice began to shout,

"Open the door! Let me out!"

Let me out!

As soon as the baker opened the oven door,

the gingerbread man jumped down to the floor...

I'm off!

and ran right out of the shop.

The baker and his wife chased him down the street, shouting, "Come back here, little ginger feet!"

But the gingerbread man just ran and ran, singing,

…a hungry boy joined the chase, calling, "Come back here, little ginger face!"

But the gingerbread man just ran and ran, singing,

*"Run, run, as fast as you can,
You can't catch me, I'm the gingerbread man!"*

Next he passed…

…a hungry cow who said, "Come back here, little ginger head!"
But the gingerbread man just ran and ran, singing,

"Run, run, as fast as you can,

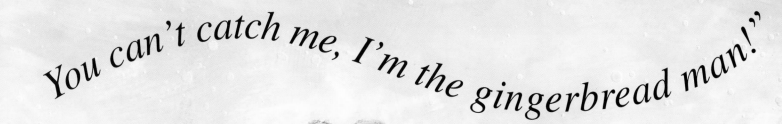

It wasn't long before he met…

…a hungry horse, neighing, "Come back here, little ginger paws!"

But the gingerbread man just ran and ran, singing,

Hey! Neigh!

"Run, run, as fast as you can, You can't catch me, I'm the gingerbread man!"

Behind him chased the horse, the cow, the boy, the baker and his wife.

In the woods hid a hungry fox. He called,
"What's the hurry, little ginger socks?"

But the gingerbread man just ran and
ran, singing,

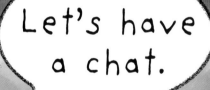

He was just thinking how clever he was, when…

…he came to a wide, wide river.

The gingerbread man stopped. He needed to think. Up crept the fox and said with a wink,

"Jump onto my tail and I'll take you across."
The gingerbread man thanked the sly fox
and he jumped onto his bushy tail.

Take care!

The fox started to swim across the wide, wide river.

Very soon he said, "Little gingerbread man, you're too heavy for my tail. Why not jump onto my red, red back?"

Faster, Foxy!

So the gingerbread man jumped onto the fox's back.

But soon the fox said, "Little gingerbread man, you're too heavy for my back. Why not hop onto my shiny, black nose?"

So the gingerbread man hopped onto the fox's nose.

Just as they came near to the bank, the fox tossed back his head.

And with a flick of his neck, he tossed the gingerbread man up, up, up in the air.

Then the gingerbread man fell
down, down, down...

SNAP! straight into the fox's gaping mouth.

And that was the end of the gingerbread man.

With a sly smile, the fox trotted home, singing,

"Run, run, as fast as you can,
But **I** caught **you**, little gingerbread man!"

Mmmm!

The Little
Red Hen

One sunny spring morning, the little red hen was scratching about the farmyard.

Suddenly…

"Look! Look!" clucked the little red hen. "I spy…

"…a grain of wheat!"

The little red hen was *very* excited! She showed it to her friends in the farmyard.

"Who will help me to plant this wheat?" she asked.

"Not I," yawned the sleepy, stripey cat.

"Not I," sniffed the sleek, skinny rat.

"Not I," snorted the plump, pink pig.

Too busy!

"Then I will plant this wheat myself," said the little red hen.

And she did.

It'll never grow.

The little red hen weeded and watered
the wheat every day.

Soon the wheat began to grow.

...and it **grew** till it was tall and golden.

"Who will help me to cut the wheat?" asked the little red hen.

"Not I," purred the preening, stripey cat.

"Not I," sang the snoozing, skinny rat.

"Not I," mumbled the muddy, pink pig.

"Then I will cut the wheat myself," said the little red hen.

And she did.

"Who will help me to take this wheat to the mill?" asked the little red hen.

"Not I," said the big, stripey cat.

"Not I," shouted the small, skinny rat.

"Not I," laughed the large, pink pig.

Too busy!

"Then I will take this wheat to the mill myself," said the little red hen.

And she did.

Round and round went the windmill as it ground the wheat.

Soon the little red hen had a big sack of fine white flour to take home.

She was very pleased!

What shall I bake?

"Who will help me to bake some bread?" asked the little red hen.

"Not I," called the curled-up, stripey cat.

"Not I," said the sneaky, skinny rat.

"Not I," giggled the gleeful, pink pig.

"Then I will bake the bread myself," said the little red hen.

And she did.

Mmmmm!

"Who will help me to eat this bread?"
asked the little red hen.

"I will!" said the eager, stripey cat. "It smells so-o-o delicious!"

"I will!" said the hungry, skinny rat. "I *love* freshly baked bread!"

"I will!" said the greedy, pink pig. "With lots of creamy butter, please!"

But the little red hen had other plans.

"Not you, stripey cat! Not you, skinny rat! Not you, greedy pig! You didn't help me at all. So now I'm going to eat this warm, fresh bread all by myself."

And she did… with *oodles* of creamy butter!

The Three
Billy Goats Gruff

Once upon a time there were three billy goats Gruff, Gruff, Gruff, who said, "This grass isn't good enough! We need to look for pastures new, where the grass is sweet and delicious to chew."

Off they trotted till they came to a river,
where they saw…

...across the water, a meadow green,
with the sweetest grass they had ever seen.

The goats longed to cross the bridge, but...

a wicked old troll lived underneath,
with horrible claws and terrible teeth,
and he gobbled up anyone trying to cross.

I'm the boss!

Soon the littlest billy goat Gruff said, "I'm off across the bridge to eat that sweet grass!"

And off he trotted with a trip trap, trip trap, across the wooden planks.

The wicked old troll sharpened his claws and gnashed his teeth, and…

I'm hungry!

…UP he popped with a monstrous growl!

"WHO'S THAT TRIP-TRAPPING ACROSS MY BRIDGE?"

"It's only me," said the littlest billy goat Gruff. "Please let me past, to eat the green grass!"

But the troll growled, "No! No! I'M going to eat YOU instead!"

I'm very hungry!

"Oh, please don't!" said the small billy goat. "Just wait a while! The second billy goat will make you smile! He's much bigger and fatter than I!"

And the troll thought, "Mmmmm… that's worth a try!"

So the littlest billy goat Gruff skipped over the bridge and into the meadow.

Soon the middle-sized billy goat Gruff said,
"I'm off across the bridge to eat that
sweet grass!"

And off he trotted with a trip trap, trip trap,
across the wooden planks.

The wicked old troll sharpened his claws and gnashed his teeth, and…

He looks tasty!

…UP he popped with a deafening roar!
"WHO'S THAT TRIP-TRAPPING ACROSS MY BRIDGE?"

"It's only me," said the middle-sized billy goat Gruff. "Please let me past, to eat the green grass!"

But the troll roared, "No! No! I'M going to eat YOU instead!"

"Oh, please don't!" said the middle-sized billy goat. "Just wait a while! The third billy goat will make you smile! He's much, much bigger and fatter than I!"

And the troll thought, "Mmmmm… that's worth a try!"

So the middle-sized billy goat Gruff skipped over the bridge and into the meadow.

Soon the big billy goat Gruff said,
"I'm off across the bridge to eat that
sweet grass!"

And off he trotted with a trip trap, trip trap,
across the wooden planks.

The wicked old troll sharpened his claws
and gnashed his teeth, and...

…UP he popped with a fearful holler!
"WHO'S THAT TRIP-TRAPPING ACROSS
MY BRIDGE?"

"It's ME!" said the big billy goat Gruff. "I'm going past to eat the green grass!"

But the troll hollered, "No! No! I'M going to eat YOU instead!"

I'M going to eat YOU!

And the third billy goat said, in a voice like thunder…

"OH NO, YOU'RE NOT!"

Down went the billy goat's head…

...SPLASH!

into the river, never to be seen again!

Then the big billy goat Gruff skipped across the bridge to join his brothers.

And the three billy goats munched happily in pastures new, saying, "Mmmmm... this grass is so good to chew!"

MUNCH!

MUNCH!

MUNCH!

The Three Little Pigs

Once upon a time, there were three little pigs. They were brave. They were bold. But they weren't very big.

One fine day the little pigs set off to see the world.

"*Always* look out for the big, bad wolf,"
said their mother. "He's bad. He's big.
And he'd love to eat a tasty little…"

The three little pigs hadn't gone far when
they met a man carrying a heavy load
of straw.

"I could build a very fine house with that straw," said the first little pig.

And he did.

The two little pigs set off, leaving their brother at his house of straw.

Before long a man came by, with sticks on his back piled ever so high.

"I could build a very fine house with those sticks," said the second little pig.

And she did.

The last little pig set off, leaving his sister at her house of sticks. Soon he met a man carrying a load of bricks.

"I could build a very fine house with those bricks," said the third little pig.

And he did.

Meanwhile, who was creeping up to the house of straw? It was…

…the big, bad wolf!

"Little pig, little pig, let me come in!"
he growled.

"No! By the hairs on my chinny chin chin,
I won't let you in!" squeaked the first
little pig.

"Then I'll HUFF and I'll PUFF

and I'll blow your house down!" roared the wolf.

Help!

And he did. That was the end of the first little pig.

Next the wolf crept up to the house of sticks.

"Little pig, little pig, let me come in!"
he growled.

"No! By the hairs on my chinny chin chin,
I won't let you in!" squeaked the second
little pig.

"Then I'll HUFF and I'll PUFF and I'll blow your house down!" roared the wolf.

Help!

And he did. That was the end of the second little pig.

Next the wolf crept up to the house of bricks.

"Little pig, little pig, let me come in!" he growled.

"No! By the hairs on my chinny chin chin, I won't let you in!" squeaked the third little pig.

So the wolf *HUFFED* and he *PUFFED*…
and he *HUFFED* and he *PUFFED*…
but he couldn't blow down the house of bricks.

"Little pig," called the wolf, "be ready at six o'clock tomorrow morning, and we'll gather some tasty turnips."

I'll be there!

The little pig knew that the wolf planned
to eat him. So off he set at *five* o'clock.
He filled his basket with tasty turnips and
hurried home before six o'clock.

"Bother!" growled the wolf.

"Little pig," called the wolf, "be ready at five o'clock tomorrow morning, and we'll pick some juicy apples."

So the little pig set off at *four* o'clock. He filled his basket with juicy apples and hurried home before five o'clock.

"BOTHER!" roared the wolf.

"Little pig," called the wolf, "be ready at four o'clock this afternoon, and we'll go to the fair."

As soon as the wolf went away, the little pig set off for the fair. He had SO much fun!

ROLL UP!
ROLL U

Suddenly the wolf fell down the chimney into the pot of boiling water with a...

CRASH! and a SPLASH!

And that was the end of the big, bad wolf.

Now the wolf was *really* angry. He climbed onto the roof.

"Little pig, I'm coming to EAT YOU UP!" he shouted down the chimney.

Indoors, the pig put a pot of water on to boil...

And the little pig said, "Now I can live happily ever after in my very fine house of bricks!"

And he did!